A GOLDEN BOOK • NEW YORK

I'm a Truck

By Dennis Shealy • Illustrated by Bob Staake

HOW-DEE!

My name's Big Blue Bill, and I'm a truck. I've got eighteen wheels turning, six hundred horses under the hood, and fifty-three feet o' trailer hanging on behind.

If there's a stretch of asphalt between Big Tuna and the Big Apple, I've ridden, rocked, bucked, and bounced down it, carrying one heavy load or another.

BIG TUNA ←

BIG APPLE →

SPEED
55
LIMIT

TOLL

CLEARANCE: 14 FEET

No.6

GAS

FOOD

TAXI

CITY CAB

CURB YOUR CAR

ROUTE
9
SOUTH

ICE CREAM
METROPOLIS
It's so yummy!
HOTEL
ROUTE 6A
STATE
55
ROUTE
CAUTION:
LOW CLEARANCE
IN TUNNEL
ONE WAY

Now, the highway is a big place to call home. On country roads, I see tractors tilling the soil and pulling special contraptions that plant seeds. Come harvest time, huge combines cut and pluck and gather up all the good food you eat.

VALLEY GRAIN CO.

Then pickups, flatbeds, and big trucks like me haul it to market.

Speaking of food, my fuel gauge is saying, "Big Blue Bill, you are *hun-greee*." When that happens, there's no place like my favorite truck stop, where I refuel and *reee*-lax.

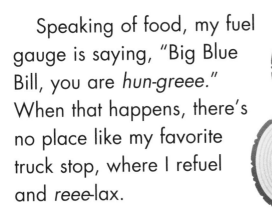

TINATOWN
GAS + FUE

Leif Co.

Hey, there's Polar Bear Pierre. He's refrigerated to keep milk and meat cold. Tanker Tina hauls gas and oil. And ol' Leif is a logging truck.

I may be the biggest truck on the road, but I'm not the only one. I can be halfway between nowhere and somewhere when along comes Bony Tony. He's a trailer truck that carries cars and small trucks to dealerships near you.

Good golly, there's Mo the tow truck. Looks
like my buddy Earl's down on his luck.
"How are ya feeling, Earl?"
"I've been better, Bill, but I'll be all right."

Detour?

Well, with all these cars and trucks
on the road, sometimes you just have to
make more road. Meet some of my biggest
buddies.

Brunhilda the bulldozer comes through first,
to clear the way. When she's finished pushing
and shoving all that dirt, she calls her buddy Dirk the
dump truck over to haul the rubble away.

Carl the grader comes along next with his wide metal blade to carve out the shape of the road. "Hey, Carl! Ya missed a spot."

Dirty Al lays the asphalt—and *ooo-wee*, that asphalt is hot, stinky, and sticky till it cools. Lazy Al is a heavy steamroller that rolls right along behind him real slow to make the asphalt smooth as mashed potatoes. No lumps. No bumps.

"Hey, boys, give me a lane, and make it double wide."

If you want to see
trucks bumper to bumper,
the city's the place to go.
But the last place I want to
be is stuck behind a garbage
truck. *Ooo-wee,* they make
Dirty Al seem downright rosy!

ROBOT TOY STORE

Pizza

...way at City Ave.

METRO
GARBAGE
COMPANY

METROPOLIS

Mini
MUFFIN
manufacturing

TAXI

TELEPHONE REPAIR
555-2303

BROADWAY

No matter what, I get out of the way
fast when I hear a siren. Fire trucks,
police cars, and ambulances have the
most important job a vehicle can have—
keeping you safe!

Firefighters put out fires with their big
pumper trucks and rescue people from
tall buildings with their ladder trucks.
Police officers direct traffic safely out
of the way. And if you get injured, you
can just bet an ambulance will get you
to the hospital mighty quick!

I love skyscrapers because my best buddies build 'em. Tipper drives around all day mixing cement. And Shorty, who's actually quite tall, lifts heavy steel beams so far into the air, my wheels get wobbly just thinking about it.

Pickups, bulldozers, backhoes, and more all work together to build buildings so tall, you'd think you could grab a piece of blue sky.

Well, here we are—the docks. It's time to drop off my load! Forklifts and cranes will put my freight on a cargo ship, and then it's off to parts unknown.

"Y'all be careful with that, now!"

As soon as I'm unloaded, I get reloaded, and then I'm off again. Those ships have an exciting life on the high seas . . .

. . . but I'm a truck and my home is the highway, so I'd best be getting down it. It's been real nice driving with ya, partner. Next time you see a truck, you tell 'im Big Blue Bill said

THE HAPPY MAN AND HIS
DUMP TRUCK

By Miryam • Illustrated by Tibor Gergely

Once upon a time there was a man who had a
dump truck. Every time he saw a friend, he would
wave his hand and tip the dumper.

One day he was riding in his dump truck,
singing a happy song, when he met a pig going
along the road.

"Would you like a ride in my dump truck?"
he asked.

"Oh, thank you!" said the pig. And he
climbed into the back of the truck.

After they had gone a little way down the road, the man saw a friend.

He waved his hand and tipped the dumper.

"Whee," said the pig. "What fun!" And
he slid all the way down to the bottom of
the dumper.

Very soon they came to a farm.

"Here is where my friends live," said the pig.
"You have a nice dump truck. Would you please let
my friends see your truck?"

"I will give them a ride in my dump truck," said
the man.

So the hen and the rooster climbed into
the truck.

And the duck climbed into the truck.

And the dog and the cat climbed into the truck.
And the pig climbed back into the truck, too.

And the man closed the tailgate, so they would
not fall out.

And then off they went.
They went past the farm, and all the animals
waved to the farmer.

The man was very happy. "They are all my
friends," he said.

So he waved his hand and tipped the dumper.

The hen, the rooster, the duck, the dog, the cat,
and the pig all slid down the dumper into a big heap!

The animals were all so happy! Then the man
took them for a long ride, and drove them back
to the farm.

He opened the tailgate wide and raised the dumper all the way up.

All the animals slid off the truck onto the ground.

"What a fine sliding board," they all said.

"Thank you," said all the animals.

"Cucka, cucka,"
clucked the hen.

"Cock-a-doodle-doo," the rooster crowed.

"Quack, quack,"
quacked the duck.

"Bow-wow,"
barked the dog.
"Meow, meow,"
mewed the cat.

And the pig let out a great big grunt,
"Oink, oink!"

The man waved his hand and tipped the
dumper, and he rode off in his dump truck,
singing a happy song.

I'm a MONSTER TRUCK

By Dennis Shealy · Illustrated by Bob Staake

I smash!

I bash!

CRASH!

I love the sound
of breaking glass!

'Cause I'm a . . .

I was *made* to make mud fly.

I may slide, but I never slip. My tall
tires GRAB the dirt . . .

as I take tight twists and extreme turns.

When I race, I race to win!

But racing isn't everything.
I'm gargantuan *and* graceful!
The freestyle event is where
I show off my smooth moves.

and they do it all
without a net!

hang
time

There's my buddy Billy Wrecks. He and his crew are part of the demolition derby.

They smash, bash, and crash each other until there's only one car left in the mud.

But don't worry—
they love it!

When the show's over, we love
to take one last lap for the crowd.

well
done!

5

Then it's lights-out!
Time for this monster truck
to stop the roarin' . . .

and start the SNORIN'!

But heck, I *am* a monster truck. And
I love to crush cars under my big wheels!

CRRRUNCH!

The more I crunch 'em, the
louder my fans cheer.

Uh-oh, looks like Carcharodontosaurus wants my leftovers. He's a monster machine that eats cars and breathes fire!

Don't worry—monster trucks aren't afraid of *anything*.

I'll put this mechanical menace back in his cage.

It's time for a break!
Let's watch the motorcycles take to the air.

They criss and they cross,
but they don't crash . . .